Teddy Bear, Teddy Bear

For Jen, Kate, and John
—A.S.

For my parents, Bill and Yvonne
—L.H.G.

Teddy Bear, Teddy Bear

Text copyright © 2003 by Alice Schertle

Illustrations copyright © 2003 by Linda Hill Griffith

Manufactured in China. All rights reserved.

www.harperchildrens.com

Library of Congress
Cataloging-in-Publication Data

Schertle, Alice.

Teddy bear, teddy bear / poems by Alice Schertle ;
paintings by Linda Hill Griffith.

p.   cm.

Summary: An illustrated collection of more than
a dozen poems that celebrate teddy bears.

ISBN 0-688-16870-1 — ISBN 0-688-16871-X (lib. bdg.)

1. Teddy bears—Juvenile poetry. 2. Children's poetry,
American. [1. Teddy bears—Poetry. 2. American poetry.]
I. Griffith, Linda Hill, ill. II. Title.

PS3569.C48435 T43 2003   2001044630

811'.54—dc21   CIP

                                                                    AC

Typography by Jeanne L. Hogle

1 2 3 4 5 6 7 8 9 10

❖

First Edition

Teddy Bear, Teddy Bear

Poems by Alice Schertle • Paintings by Linda Hill Griffith

HarperCollinsPublishers

Teddy Bear Store

Bears in striped pajamas,
Bears in running shoes.
Miles of bears. Piles of bears.
Care for a bear? Just choose.

Teddy bears of every kind,
Bears with pull strings,
Bears you wind,
Bears that roller-skate,
Bears that sing,
Bears that don't do anything.

Small bears on the top shelves,
Big bears on the bottom.
Piles of bears. Miles of bears.
Care for a bear? We've got 'em.

Middle-Sized Bear

Here's a middle-sized bear, not big, not small,
and not too short—but not too tall.
His ears are thin, but his tummy is fat,
he's a little bit this way,
a little bit that.
He's sort of quiet when he doesn't act wild—
he'd be just the bear
for a middle-sized child
who's sometimes fast and sometimes slow
and high sometimes when she's not down low,
who comes inside when she doesn't stay out
and talks in a whisper when she doesn't shout.
If a child like that is a little like you,
a bear like this is the bear
for you.

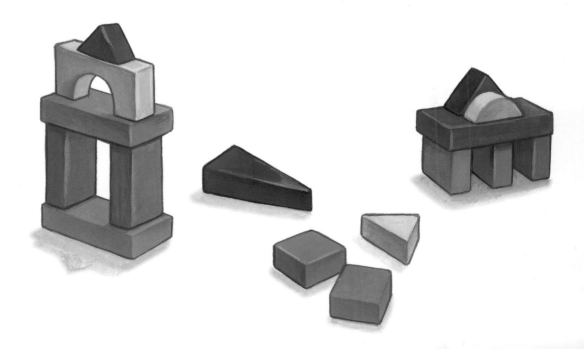

Banister Bears

Bears on the staircase
all in a row,
bears on the banister—
LOOK OUT BELOW!

WHOOSH! SWOOSH!
Slippery steep!
Banister bears—
       all

              in

                   a

                      heap!

Scrub-a-Dub

Dirty brown bear
Mixing-bowl tub
Scrub-a-dub-dub
Scrub-a-dub-dub
   Towel wrap
   Powder nose
   Underwear
   Clean clothes
   Blow-dry
   Puff hair

Oh, my!

Beautiful bear!

A Bad Bear Day

The teddy bear's pinching the zebra,
Koala Bear's poking the cat,
the panda said, "Shoo!" to the mouse and the gnu,
and stamped on the elephant's hat.

The black bear is teasing the tiger,
the brown bear called Piggy "*a mess!*"
Blueberry Bear pulled Orangutan's hair—
it's just a bad bear day, I guess.

My Bear

Doesn't have elbows, doesn't have knees.
No teeth. No fingers. No toes.
Has arms, has legs, has ears and eyes,
fuzzy fat tummy, sewed-on nose—
and Me to dress him in some of my clothes:

    earmuffs

    underpants

    dinosaur socks

and take him wherever he goes.

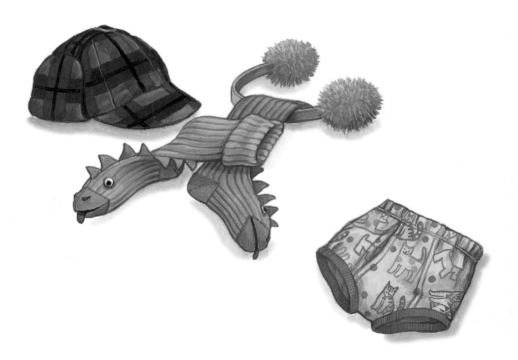

Please Do Not Stare

Please do not stare
at the polar bear
who is reading a book at the zoo.
He does not care
for people who look
over his shoulder. Would you?

Please do not stare
at the grizzly bear
who is chewing your shoes and your socks.
You should have known
to leave him alone—
never open a grizzly bear box!

Please do not stare
at the teddy bear
who is sound asleep in my lap.
    He has fallen asleep
    the way teddy bears do,
    he'll be here in my lap
    for an hour or two,
    and he'll pick up his toys
    as soon as he's through—
but *now* he is taking a *nap*!

Teddy Bear, Teddy Bear

Teddy bear, teddy bear, almost asleep.
Kitty cat, kitty cat, coming a-creep
closer . . . closer . . . closer . . . LEAP!

Drat!
Just like a cat!

Mostly

Teddy bears
     are mostly brown
     or white, or blue
     or green (a few)
but mostly brown.

Teddy bears
     are mostly small
     (for prizes
     there are larger sizes)
but mostly small.

Teddy bears
     are mostly quiet
     seldom shout
     or bang about.
Just mostly quiet.

Teddy bears
     are mostly stout
     unless their stuffing's
     leaking out
which makes them thin.

If you should find
     a teddy bear
     please take him in.

Pumpernickel Bear

Pumpernickel Bear
with ketchup in his hair
and a smudge of mashed potato on his nose,
eats his dinner up completely
but he doesn't do it neatly
and he wipes his sticky paws off
on his clothes.
And I know (because I've seen it)
that he licks the plate to clean it—
and then puts it in the cupboard, I suppose.

Teddy Bear Wear

A fireman bear wears waterproof boots
    and a big red fireman's hat.
A teddy policeman pins on a badge
    (he looks more official like that).
Teddy bear ballerinas
    wear tutus and pink satin slippers.
Teddy bear divers wear Speedos and goggles
    and earplugs and air tanks and flippers.

But sometimes a teddy bear just wants to be
a regular warm sort of bear
that somebody might want to cuddle and
squeeze—
    a hug is the best thing to wear.

Bears on the Bus

(A Crocodile's Complaint)

Bears on the bus,
hanging on to the straps,
sitting three to a seat,
piled on other bears' laps—
there isn't a smidgen of room left for *us*
because there are so many
bears on the bus!

Bears on the bus
get *pushy* and *crowdy*,
they whistle and sing
and begin to act rowdy.

I seldom complain,
I don't like to fuss—
but why are there so many
bears on the bus?

Barely Bear

Barely Bear
barely there,
lost his hat,
lost his hair.

Windup key
wound up broken.
Lost his voice.
Hasn't spoken

since July.
Clothes are missing.
Lost his nose
(too much kissing).

Wrinkles, lumps,
patches, creases—
Barely Bear's
been loved to pieces.

Little Bear Sleeping

Moon peeks over a distant hill.
Wind comes rattling as the old wind will.
"Hush," says the moon, "be still, be still—
there's a little bear sleeping on the windowsill."